For Kasia
A.J.B

To duck lovers
Irene and Cesare
F.C.

First published in Great Britain in 2010 by Gullane Children's Books
This edition published in 2011 by
Gullane Children's Books
185 Fleet Street, London, EC4A 2HS
www.gullanebooks.com

1 3 5 7 9 10 8 6 4 2

A CIP record for this title is available from the British Library.

ISBN: 978-1-86233-812-8

Printed and bound in China

Love-a-Duck

Alan James Brown

illustrated by Francesca Chessa

A little girl named Jane had a yellow
plastic duck called Love-a-Duck.
She played with him in the bath
and he was always clean and shiny.
He loved Jane and was very happy.

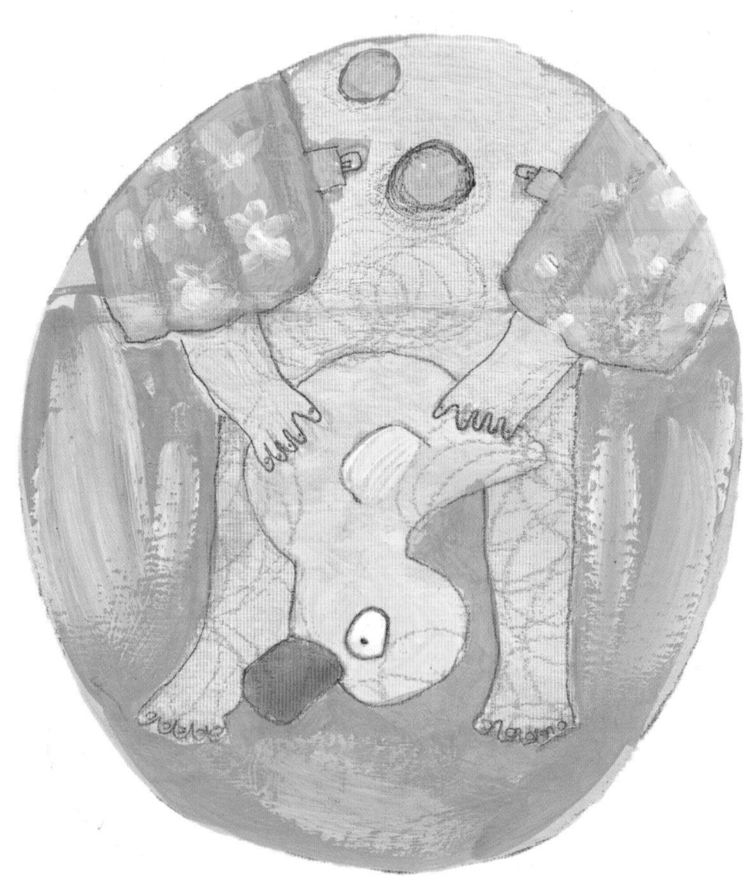

Jane pushed Love-a-Duck under
the water and let him bounce up . . .

She squeezed soapy water out of him. Love-a-Duck tried to squeak, but all he could say was . . .

"squirt, squirt!"

"Oh Love-a-Duck!" said Jane. "You can't even squeak!" Love-a-Duck felt very sad. He thought that Jane didn't love him anymore.

Mum put Love-a-Duck on the window sill
while she cleaned the bath. He was so full of water
that he toppled over and fell out of the window.
Did anybody see?

No, they didn't!

Love-a-Duck landed in . . .

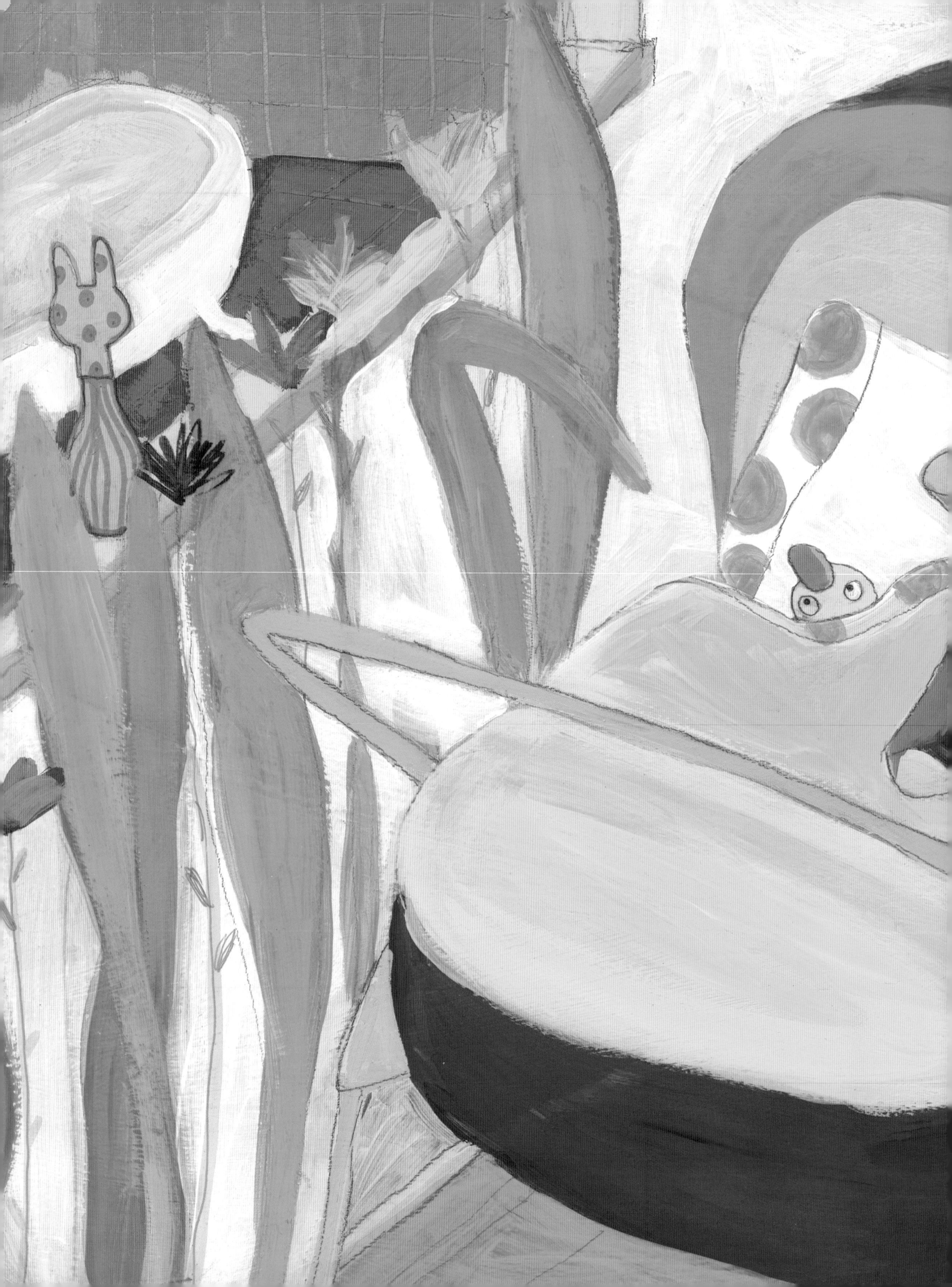

John's pram.

Love-a-Duck wanted
to get out of the pram, but
he got lost under the blankets.
He tried to squeak, but
all he could say was . . .

"Squidge, squidge!"

Mum and Jane came out with Buster the Dog,
and together they pushed John's pram down the road.
Did anybody know that Love-a-Duck was in the pram with John?

No, they didn't!

At the park, Jane played on the swings. Mum lifted John out of the pram and Love-a-Duck

fell out . . .

and then . . .

Buster the Dog grabbed
him in his jaws and ran away.
Did anybody see?

No, they didn't!

All the bath water was squeezed out
of Love-a-Duck. He tried to squeak,
but all he could say was,
"squoo, squoo!"

Buster saw the ducks on the pond.
He opened his jaws to bark and
Love-a-Duck fell into the water.
Did anybody see?

No, they didn't!

The wind blew Love-a-Duck across the pond.
He thought he was swimming, like a real duck.

He tried to squeak, but all he could say was . . .

"squark, squark!"

It was like the noise the real ducks made – almost! Was he turning into a real duck?

"Real ducks dibble in the mud,"
said the ducks, and they splashed Love-a-Duck
with mud until only his eyes were showing.
He tried to squeak but all he could say was . . .

"Squish, Squish!"

The ducks laughed at Love-a-Duck.
Then they flapped their wings and flew away.
Love-a-Duck tried to fly, but his wings didn't work.
He was stuck in the middle of the pond –
and felt very sad.

Love-a-Duck tried to swim, but he just turned upside down in the water. And as the fish pushed him back to the side of the pond he tried to squeak, but all he could say was . . .

"Squubble, squubble!"

Jane was at the
top of the slide.
Did she see him?

No, she didn't!

"Time to go home!" said Mum.
Would anyone ever
see Love-a-Duck?

Yes! At last,
somebody saw him.

Buster the Dog grabbed Love-a-Duck in his jaws and carried him out of the park following Mum and Jane. Love-a-Duck tried to squeak, but all he could say was,

"squoo, squoo!"

At home, Mum said, "Hot baths for everyone!"
Jane sat at one end of the bath, John at the other,
then Buster put his head over the side and . . .

Love-a-Duck fell into the water!
At once he was clean and shiny again.
Did Jane see him?

Yes, this time . . . she did!

"Love-a-Duck!" said Jane. "You're my best toy!"
Love-a-Duck was so happy!
He loved Jane, and he loved being her toy.
Jane pushed Love-a-Duck under the water.
She let him go and he bounced up,

BOING!

Jane squeezed him.
Loud and clear, Love-a-Duck said . . .

"squeak

squeak!"

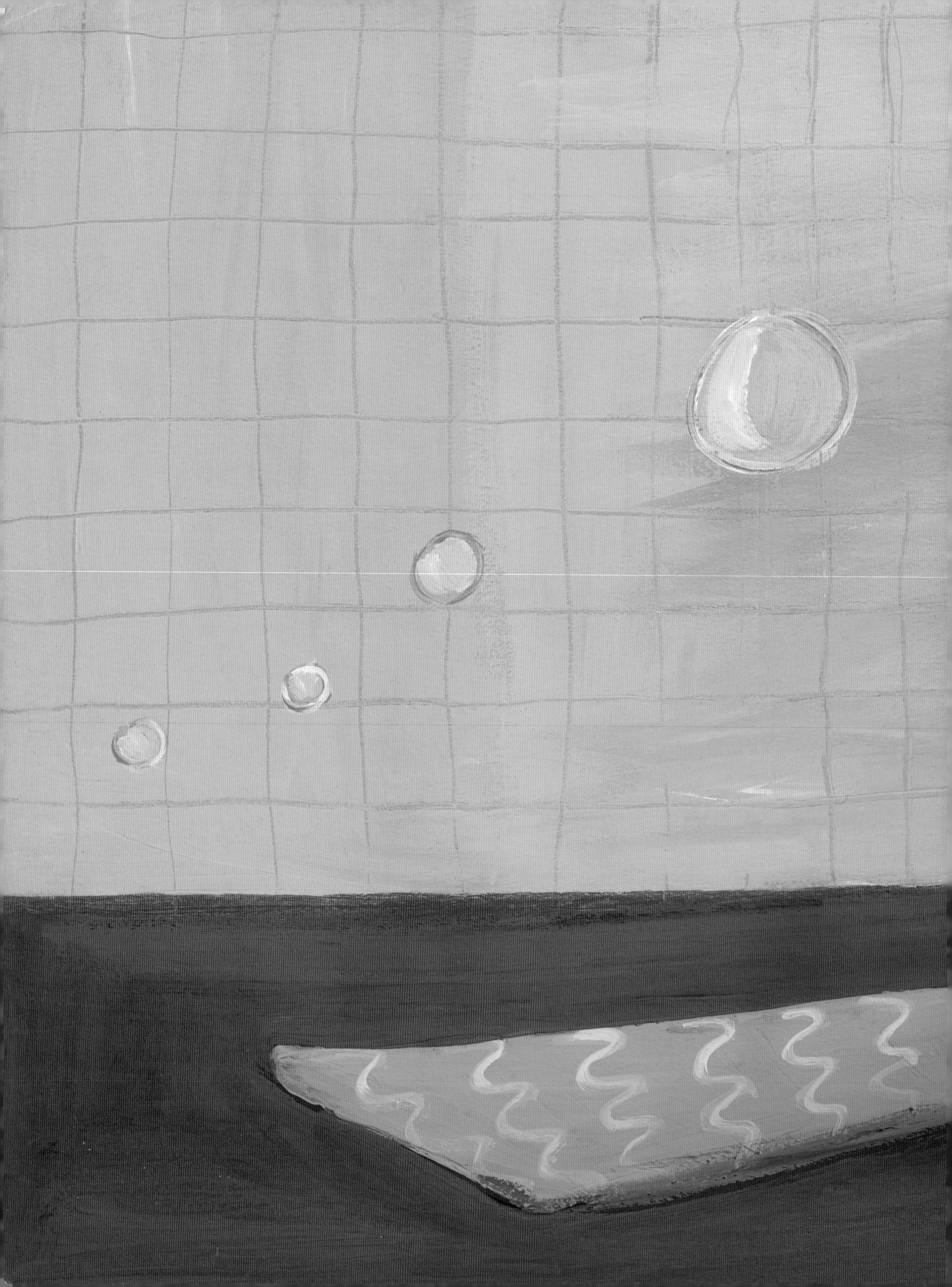